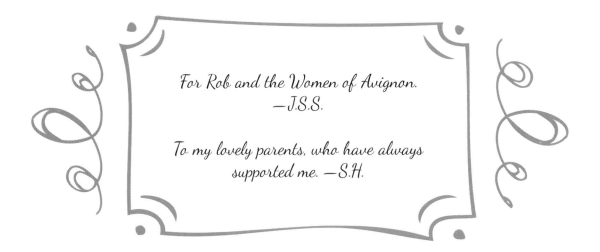

For Rob and the Women of Avignon.
—J.S.S.

To my lovely parents, who have always
supported me. —S.H.

Published by Familius™ LLC, www.familius.com

Familius books are available at special discounts for bulk purchases, whether for sales promotions
or for family or corporate use. For more information, contact Premium Sales at 559-876-2170 or
email orders@familius.com.

Library of Congress Cataloging-in-Publication Data
2016942211   ISBN 9781942934714

Printed in China

Book and jacket design by David Miles
Edited by Lindsay Sandberg and Trish Madson

10 9 8 7 6 5 4 3 2 1

First Edition

12 Little Elves visit WASHINGTON

BY JESS SMART SMILEY

ILLUSTRATIONS BY SADIE HAN

FAMILIUS

'Twas Christmas in Washington,
and twelve elves were sent
to see who was sleeping . . .

away the elves went!

In each home was nestled each girl and each boy,
while visions of Washington brought everyone joy.

The Space Needle rose
through the fog and the rain,

and the red salmon swam
past the boats and the trains.

The Museum of Glass
shimmered and shone,

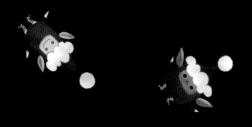

and the Great Wheel spun
'round its Seattle home.

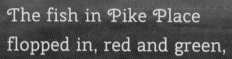

The fish in Pike Place
flopped in, red and green,

PIKE PLACE

MAR KET

and Mount Rainier dressed
in a wintry scene.

The Hoh Rainforest was quiet,
not a sound to be heard
except for the singing
of one goldfinch bird.

The Fremont Troll snuggled
under the bridge.
He kept one eye open
(but no more than a smidge).

The World's Fair Pavilion lit up the whole night
with colors so beautiful, vivid, and bright.

Climbers on Rainier
and Saint Helens hikers
enjoyed the winter
with campers and bikers.

The carousel spun
'round Riverfront Park
as the sky changed from white
to pink to dark.

Goodnight, Washington.
You're all fast asleep,
but there's just one more house
that the elves want to see . . .

Hurry to bed and shut your eyes tight.
Merry Christmas, dear Washington.
Twelve elves say goodnight!